Your Turn

Written by Megan Borgert-Spaniol

Illustrated by Lisa Hunt

GRL Consultants, Diane Craig and Monica Marx,
Certified Literacy Specialists

Lerner Publications ◆ Minneapolis

Note from a GRL Consultant
This Pull Ahead leveled book has been carefully designed for beginning readers. A team of guided reading literacy experts has reviewed and leveled the book to ensure readers pull ahead and experience success.

Lerner Publications Company
An imprint of Lerner Publishing Group, Inc.
241 First Avenue North
Minneapolis, MN 55401 USA

For reading levels and more information, look up this title at www.lernerbooks.com.

Main body text set in Mikado 24/41
Typeface provided by Hannes von Doehren.

The images in this book are used with the permission of: Lisa Hunt

Library of Congress Cataloging-in-Publication Data

Names: Borgert-Spaniol, Megan, 1989- author. | Hunt, Lisa, 1973- illustrator.
Title: Your turn / Megan Borgert-Spaniol, Lisa Hunt.
Description: Minneapolis, MN : Lerner Publications, 2022. | Series: Be a good sport (pull ahead readers people smarts - fiction) | Includes index. | Audience: Ages 4–7 | Audience: Grades K–1 | Summary: "Lola and Lupe take turns going first when playing on the slide, and wait patiently for their turn to use the swings. Pairs with the nonfiction title Playing Fair"— Provided by publisher.
Identifiers: LCCN 2021010317 (print) | LCCN 2021010318 (ebook) | ISBN 9781728440989 (library binding) | ISBN 9781728444383 (ebook)
Subjects: LCSH: Sharing—Juvenile literature.
Classification: LCC BJ1533.G4 B67 2022 (print) | LCC BJ1533.G4 (ebook) | DDC 177/.7—dc23

LC record available at https://lccn.loc.gov/2021010317
LC ebook record available at https://lccn.loc.gov/2021010318

Manufactured in the United States of America
1 – CG – 12/15/21

Table of Contents

Your Turn

Lola and Lupe went to the park.
"You go first," said Lola.
Lupe climbed up the ladder.

"Your turn," said Lupe.

Lola climbed up the ladder.

"You go first," said Lupe.

Lola went down the slide.

"Your turn," said Lola.

Lupe went down the slide.

Lola and Lupe waited for the swings.

"Our turn!" they said.

What is a way you can play fairly with your friends?

Did You See It?

ladder

slide

swings

Index